T0284104

FATAL FORTUNE

CAROLYN RIDDER ASPENSON

SEVERN RIVER
PUBLISHING

Severn River Publishing
www.SevernRiverBooks.com

This is a work of fiction. Names, characters, businesses, places, events and incidents are either the products of the author's imagination or used in a fictitious manner. Any resemblance to actual persons, living or dead, or actual events is purely coincidental.

ISBN: 978-1-64875-331-2 (Paperback)

ALSO BY CAROLYN RIDDER ASPENSON

The Rachel Ryder Thriller Series

Damaging Secrets

Hunted Girl

Overkill

Countdown

Body Count

Fatal Silence

Deadly Means

To find out more about Carolyn Ridder Aspenson and her books, visit

severnriverbooks.com/authors/carolyn-ridder-aspenson

For Jack
For always believing in me

1

Spring in Georgia was different from spring in Chicago. Back home, I'd wear shorts and a sweatshirt in late March. I froze my ass off, but spring had sprung, and Chicagoans celebrated with shorts, even if that meant frostbite.

Come spring in Georgia, and residents still walked around in sweaters and jeans, complaining about the weather as they wiped their noses. Though it was a beautiful season with flowers and trees blooming in stunningly bright colors, that beauty created an evil villain called pollen, which turned everything in its path yellow.

That wasn't an exaggeration. Yesterday I'd walked outside the department and stood in shock. Every car in the lot wore a covering of yellow at least a half inch thick. I sneezed my way to my vehicle and quickly drove to CVS for a bottle of allergy medicine.

The medicine helped, but I'd lost my voice anyway. I woke up for my late shift and sounded like Demi Moore when I greeted my fish. Okay, *that* was an exaggeration. My scratchy, twelve-year-old-boy-going-through-puberty voice resembled that of a sick cow, but saying Demi Moore gave me confidence.

I'd stopped at Dunkin' Donuts for a large coffee, thinking the warm liquid would ease the pain of my raw throat. I even picked up a cup for my partner, Rob Bishop. I walked into his cubby and placed the coffee in front of him on his desk.

"Wow." He smiled up at me. "Are we going steady now?"

"When did you last date? The fifties? No one says 'going steady' anymore." I cleared my throat. "But no, we're not. You're too old for me, Dad."

"That would hurt my ego if you didn't sound like a dying animal. Why didn't you call in?" He turned to the file cabinet behind him, opened a drawer, and removed something too small for me to see. He handed it to me. "This will help your throat."

"Thanks. I'll give it a shot after I finish my coffee."

We'd begun working together several months back, when I'd moved from Chicago to an Atlanta suburb called Hamby. I'd moved thinking I'd have a lighter schedule, and I had, but the calls we took had been mundane ones involving entitled teenagers committing stupid crimes, until a big case came along and yours truly busted it wide open. I wasn't trying to brag. I was just grateful to be busy. Busy was good, after all. It kept me from thinking about things I didn't need or want to think about.

An officer knocked on Bishop's cubby partition. "We had a call. Shots fired. Chief wants you two on it."

I'd dressed in my usual gear before leaving the house, but I checked my gun anyway. Habit. "Was anyone injured?"

"One. Caller said he's dead. Ambulance is en route." He handed Bishop a piece of paper. "It's all over our channel, but here's the address." He placed his hands on his hips. "It's the Hansard house."

Bishop raised an eyebrow. "Do they know who the victim is?"

"Jeremiah Hansard."

Bishop exhaled. "Oh, hell."

"What's the Hansard house, and who's Jeremiah Hansard?"

"I'll explain in the car," Bishop said. He pointed to the officer. "Thanks for the advanced notice."

"Sure thing, Detective." The officer trotted away.

Bishop drove. Usually, one partner handled the driving on the regular, and we'd fallen into the habit of it being him. He said I drove like someone from Chicago, weaving in and out of traffic, holding a fist pressed into my horn, flipping the other driver the finger with the other hand, and cussing like a sailor. I'd learned all of that in high school driver's education, and I didn't see a problem with any of it.

"So, who's the guy, and why does his house have a name?" I asked.

"You know that house off Birmingham? The one with the big iron fence."

"The house you can't see from the road?"

He nodded. "It's the Hansard house. They've owned it since forever. The original home, which is now a guest house, was built during the Civil War. Benjamin Hansard built it as a getaway from the city. History said he wanted to keep his family safe. It's been passed down for years, but about thirty years ago, Jeremiah Hansard built the mansion, and he's lived in it ever since." He drove through the intersection. "Jeremiah is a bit of an eccentric, and he's been a shut-in since his wife passed fifteen years ago."

"Sounds like a reason to be a shut-in." I stared out the window, lost in thoughts I'd hoped to forget.

"Ryder? You okay?"

I nodded. "I'm fine."

He chuckled. "When my ex said she was fine, I knew she meant the opposite."

"Thankfully, I'm not your ex."

He smiled. "You have no idea."

The drive down Birmingham always gave me something new to admire. The street housed large lots, most five acres minimum, with mansion-sized homes, ornate gated entrances, and even a few with small horse stables. The Hansard house didn't have horses, but the gate topped the list of most ornate gates in Hamby, Georgia.

"What's with the elaborate iron gates? Is it a wealth identifier or something?"

"Not officially, but I'd say the more obnoxious the gate, the more money the family has."

"Then this Hansard guy has a lot."

"Last I heard, he was worth something like twenty-two billion, but it's probably changed."

"Holy shit! Someone's going to make bank on his will." I regretted that the minute it slipped from my lips. "Oh, that was awful. My apologies."

Bishop laughed. Partners didn't get offended by sarcasm, especially when it had to do with murder. Cops used sarcasm as a defense mechanism. We couldn't do the job if we let the bad things reach and settle too far into our souls. Those that did ended up on the wrong side of a gun or a bottle of liquor on the daily.

"He's got a great-grandniece and great-grandson, but that's about it. I think they might have had a falling out, though. I'm not sure." He parked his vehicle at the front of the circular driveway behind the ambulance.

The medical examiner had arrived just before us. "Detectives. Sorry to have to see you."

"Mike," Bishop said. They shook. "Always a pleasure."

I shook his hand as well. "Not a pleasure for me, but you get that." I smiled.

"I sure do."

"You're here early," Bishop said. "What gives?"

"My mother-in-law is in town. I paid the dispatch officer to call me if anything that might need me came in."

I laughed. "Wow. She must be some mother-in-law."

"I'll teach you all the tricks if you ever get married."

Again. If I ever got married again.

We snapped on latex gloves, and just inside the door, slipped our shoes into booties. Both matched what Barron wore during autopsies.

Officer Michels, the patrol officer who'd answered the call, met us in the foyer. I gasped and was awed at the massive space. The marble floor alone cost more than my townhouse. Probably double for all I knew. The winding stairs on both sides of the room rounded up to an expansive second floor that opened in the center but also extended down hallways on both sides of the stairs. I'd thought the iron gate was ornate, but the railing and spindles of the staircase were one hundred times more. Painted portraits hung along the walls up the stairs. The kind with miserable-looking people who either needed a drink or needed to get laid to put a smile on their faces.

Why didn't people smile in those things? Were they just generally unhappy and wanted to portray that for posterity?

"He's in the office," Michels said. He pointed to a hallway just past the foyer on the left. "Two doors down on the right."

"Find the weapon?" Bishop asked.

He shook his head. "Not yet."

I didn't know Michels well, but he seemed like a decent guy. He had a thick black mustache that reminded me of something a 70s porn star might sport. Not that I watched the stuff, but I knew the look. I'd teased him about it a few times. It was hard not to, but he took it in stride. I'd been putting in a concentrated effort to get to know some of the patrol, but many were still too good old boy enough to accept me. If they did, they did. If they didn't, that was fine with me as well.

Bishop's eyes shifted to the room on our left and the five people sitting in it. "Who're they, and why are they in the same room?"

"I have two officers in there making sure they don't talk to each other. This house is massive. If I put them in separate rooms, and one of them is the killer, he or she could have easily escaped. We don't have enough patrol here to help."

"Valid point," I said.

"Agreed," Bishop said.

Michels flipped through his small spiral notepad. "Mr. Thomas Collins—"

I interrupted him with a laugh. "Really?"

He angled his head to the side. "What?"

"Thomas Collins? Tom Collins? The drink?"

Michels shrugged. "Hadn't thought about that."

Bishop whispered in my ear. "I think he's just twenty-one."

"Twenty-six," he said. He glanced back at the notepad after rolling his eyes at my partner. "Thomas Collins, age fifty-seven, butler."

People still had butlers. Amazing.

"Great-niece Jessica Hansard, age twenty-three. House-keeper Mary Smith, age fifty-four. Landscape manager Jimmy Corbin, age thirty-six, and great-grandson Jared Hansard, age twenty-seven."

Bishop nodded. "Did you get statements?"

"I'm working on it, sir."

"We'll be in the victim's office."

"Yes, sir."

We headed toward the hallway. I nearly tripped over my own feet, gawking at the expensive and ugly vases and knick-knacks displayed everywhere. I dragged my fingers over a narrow table with dog figurines crowded on it. I smiled when I checked my finger and didn't see any dust. The housekeeper must have worked twenty-four-seven to keep the place spotless.

Dr. Barron stood in front of Jeremiah Hansard's desk. Blood from the victim's head had splattered against the wood paneling and bookcases behind him, splashing across most of the books and knickknacks on the shelves.

I walked into the room and made note of the fact that there were no family photos anywhere in the room.

Ashley Middleton, the department's only crime scene tech, stepped into the room. She set her large metal equipment case to the side just outside in the hall. Ashley was a true professional. She knew her stuff, and we'd become friends of sorts. She was younger than me, but that didn't matter. We shared the desire for truth and a love for football. Granted, she'd chosen the wrong team, but any team was wrong if it wasn't the Chicago Bears.

"Wow," she said. "It's really him." She stretched a latex glove over one hand. It snapped into place just over her wrist. The other glove did the same. She sighed. "I have a serious love/hate relationship with my job."

"You and me both," I said.

Ashley nodded. "Dr. Barron, when you're ready, just let me know. I'll start on the scene."

"Will do," he said.

I studied the victim. "Close-range shot." I moved closer to the victim. "Hands on the desk. He knew who shot him."

"No defensive movement," Bishop added.

"Right, and if I had to guess, I'd say it's your everyday nine-millimeter bullet. A nine-millimeter travels at over a thousand feet per second. The velocity is too fast for the head to react."

"My thoughts as well," Barron said. "If the muzzle were held to his head, the blast would have pushed the head back, and that's not the case."

"Right," I said. I examined the trajectory of the splatter while swallowing back the bile seeping up my throat. I'd learned to set aside my emotions at crime scenes, especially murders, but brain matter and blood splatter couldn't be unseen, and I'd always needed a moment to process what that meant to the family when they walked in and found their loved one dead.

It wasn't a suicide. A shot through the eye was a rare and complicated suicide shot, but they did happen. I'd yet to see one and, honestly, hoped I never would. Based on the splatter, it was clear he'd been shot in his seat, but Ashley would measure the spots for the record.

After a quick review of the scene, we got to the important parts: theorizing and then interviewing the suspects. Michels filled us in on what he'd learned, which wasn't much. The family and staff weren't interested in talking unless it was to ask to call their attorneys.

"Did you tell them they're not under arrest?" Bishop asked.

"Yes, sir," Michels said. "Didn't seem to matter."

"No one's changed clothes or washed their hands?" I asked.

"No clothes changed, and I'm assuming no one's used the bathroom."

"Who discovered Mr. Hansard?" Bishop asked.

"Mr. Collins, the butler."

I mumbled, "The butler, with a gun, in the office."

A smile pulled at the corners of Bishop's mouth.

"I'm sorry?" Michels asked.

I pressed my lips together. I didn't want to seem hard and emotionless at a murder scene, because I wasn't. "Have you ever played the game Clue?"

Michels tilted his head to the side. "I think I've heard of it."

I dipped my head back, sighed, and then said, "God, I'm old."

"How do you think I feel?" Bishop asked.

"Older."

He nodded.

"Let's get Ashley down to run GSR tests on the suspects," Bishop said.

Michels nodded. "I'll grab her and send her down with the kit right now."

2

Bishop took the lead on the suspects, first answering their questions with minimal information, then explaining we'd be interviewing them separately.

"How long will this take?" Jessica Hansard asked. "I have dinner plans."

I stopped myself from rolling my eyes. Her great-uncle's brain was plastered all over his books, and she wanted to eat dinner? "You can cancel your plans, Miss Hansard. It's going to be a while before you're released. If you're released at all."

Her eyes widened. "Excuse me? You mean I might have to stay here?" She stopped her entitled foot on the marble floor. "That's stupid."

Bishop dragged his hand down his overgrown razor stubble. "We're investigating a death, a possible murder. There's nothing stupid about it."

Ashley tested each person for gunshot residue. A swipe over their hands and clothing would determine if any of them had recently fired a weapon, but we wouldn't know if the weapon was the one used to kill Hansard.

"They all have it on them?" Bishop asked. "How is that possible?"

"Maybe they held the gun together?" Ashley asked.

I dropped my head to the side and said, "Well?"

"Yeah, that's a long shot. I get it."

I smiled. "It's possible they've all fired a gun today."

"Possible, but unlikely," Bishop said.

I nodded. "We'll just have to find out."

"There's something else," Ashley said. "No one has any blood splatter on their clothing."

"Really?" Bishop asked. "Maybe the killer covered him- or herself before shooting Hansard?"

"I doubt it," I said. "It's possible for someone to shoot someone at close range and not get blood on their clothing, especially when the bullet exits through the back of the head."

"Really?" Ashley asked. "I'd not heard that."

"A 2011 study inspired by Lana Clarkson's murder proved it's possible. When a gun's fired, propellant gases from the gunpowder release at high-speed, creating a vortex of some sort. That vortex basically stops any blood from the victim flying forward."

"How do you know that stuff?" Ashley asked.

"She doesn't have a social life," Bishop said.

"He's not wrong," I said.

We walked back into the room as Ashley headed back upstairs.

I escorted Mary Smith into the parlor room across the hall and closed the large wood doors behind us. Bishop had taken Tom Collins down the hall. "Ms. Smith," I said. "What is it you do for Mr. Hansard?"

"I'm his house manager. Most people consider me a house-keeper, but I'm more than that. I do maintain the home, with the help of others, when necessary, but mostly I manage the home and Mr. Hansard's personal business."

"Personal business?"

"Yes, I pay his bills, handle home repairs with vendors, those kinds of things. It's more than a housekeeper, which is why he gave me the house manager title."

"Can you tell me exactly what happened here today?"

She wiped a stray brown hair from the side of her face, then twisted her hands into a ball on her lap. Her leg bounced up and down. "I arrived for work this morning at eight thirty like I always do. Mr. Hansard was eating breakfast. I'd prepared him a spinach, ham, and cheese omelet last night before leaving. He likes to eat early, so I pre-make his breakfast, and he heats it up when he's ready to eat. If I'm there and he hasn't eaten, I do it for him."

She spoke of the deceased in the present tense, which was sometimes a sign of innocence. Sociopaths could do that without a second thought, but most people weren't sociopaths.

"How was his temperament?"

"He was his usual self." She exhaled. "Mr. Hansard isn't the kindest man, but he softens when he gets to know you. I've worked with him for twenty-five years, and we'd become rather close. So, our greeting was cheerful."

"Did you talk or just say hello?"

"We chatted like we always do."

Dragging information out of people was like pulling teeth without Novocaine. "And what was said?"

"We talked about his schedule for the day. He never goes anywhere, of course, but the doctor was supposed to come later this evening. Oh dear. I should call his office and cancel that appointment, shouldn't I?"

I handed her my notepad. "Write down his name, and we'll make sure to get in touch with him."

I asked her several more questions and then went in for the tough stuff. "Ms. Smith, when our tech wiped your hands, she found gunpowder residue on them. Can you explain why?"

"Yes, because I touched him to check his pulse. Also, it is my responsibility to clean Mr. Hansard's gun collection once a month. I was in the process of doing just that when I heard the gunshot."

"How many guns does Mr. Hansard own?"

She closed her eyes for a moment. "Thirty-three, I believe."

I forced my face not to show any emotion. "How many of them did you clean today?"

She sniffled. "I'd only gotten to seven of them when, you know." She sniffled again.

I handed her a tissue from the box on the table behind me. "Can you show me them?"

She stood. "Of course. They're in the locked room between the kitchen and dining room. I have the key."

"Does anyone else have a key?"

She nodded. "Mr. Hansard. He carried it on him with his house keys."

A female scream echoed through the hall. I looked over at Mary Smith.

She shook her head. "It's Jessica. I don't mean to be disrespectful, but she's a drama queen."

"Don't you touch me!" Jessica screamed. I recognized her voice then. "I want to call my lawyer! Now!"

"Oh, hell." I pinched the bridge of my nose. Lawyers created complications, and complications slowed investigations. We didn't have time for either of those.

Mary Smith giggled. "She's got a surprise coming."

"I'm sorry?"

We walked through the dining room into the back room, which connected to the kitchen.

"I'm the executor of Mr. Hansard's will. Upon his death, all money and payment for family providers such as attorneys, accountants, and mental health providers ceased. Once she contacts the attorney and tells him what's happened, he'll tell her he can't help her."

That would burn. "Do you have a copy of the will?"

She removed a set of keys from her pocket and opened the gun cabinet. "It's right here." She stretched to the back of the cabinet and removed a file from a pocket attached to the steel back.

I removed another pair of gloves from my pocket and snapped them on. "Please step away from the cabinet." I opened the will and gave it a quick read-through, searching for Jessica's and Jared's names. I noticed Mr. Hansard's signature on the bottom and Mary Smith's as his witness. I saw nothing left to his living relatives, only to Mary Smith and The Sunshine House in town. Why would he leave two million dollars to an employee and not his kids?

Mary stood a few feet away from the cabinet, rubbing her hands. Her eyes darted down to the floor, then to each side. She hadn't looked at me since I'd opened the will. I stuffed the papers back into the file folder. I held off asking her any questions, knowing I'd need to address it carefully given her financial benefit since Mr. Hansard's demise.

Each gun had a specific, labeled spot on a revolving rack. I scanned through them slowly. All of them were there except for a nine-millimeter Luger. "Was the Luger here when you cleaned the guns?"

"I hadn't made it to that section, so I can't be sure."

"What did you do when you heard the shot?"

"I ran to his office, of course."

"Did you see anyone near there?"

She nodded. "Everyone here. We all heard it and ran to see what happened."

"Who was there first?"

"I'm not sure. I think the only person to arrive after me was Jimmy because he came from outside."

"Tell me exactly what happened when you arrived at his office."

"Well, let's see. Jessica was standing in the hallway, screaming. Jared was in the office with Mr. Hansard, and Thomas was on his phone calling 911. I rushed in and checked Mr. Hansard's pulse, though I knew he was gone."

"How long was it before the officer arrived?"

"Oh, gosh. It wasn't long. Maybe five minutes?"

"And what happened during the time between finding Mr. Hansard and the officer arriving?"

"Thomas and Jared argued. Thomas wanted everyone out of the room, but Jared refused to leave. Thomas finally stopped pressing when Jared threatened him."

"Jared threatened him?"

She nodded. "Jared is hot-tempered. He and Mr. Hansard had problems because of it."

I'd get to that in a minute. "And Jessica and Mr. Corbin?"

"Jessica continued to scream and cry in the hallway." She closed her eyes again. I realized she did that when she needed to concentrate. "Jimmy wasn't there. He must have left after we called 911." She nodded. "But he returned at some point, because when your officer arrived, he was the one who let him in."

"What kind of problems did Mr. Hansard have with Jared?"

"Well, for starters, he thought Jared was a brat. He hasn't

worked a day in his life and has been living off Mr. Hansard since his parents died."

"When was that?"

"Two years ago. They were in a plane crash. God rest their souls."

"Was he left anything from them?"

"I assume so, but I wasn't privy to what," she said.

I played dumb about what I'd read in Mr. Hansard's will. I wanted to see how she would address it. "I only scanned Mr. Hansard's will to check for a date and notary seal. Have you seen it?"

"Yes."

"Great. Do you know if Jared is in it?"

She looked down at the floor and then back up at me. "No, not anymore, and he's going to be hell on wheels when he finds out."

"What about his great-grandniece?"

She shook her head.

"Who is in the will?" I asked.

"Well, I am, and Mr. Collins was before, but Mr. Hansard had me contact his lawyer to remove him. He'd just returned the updated document a few days ago."

"Why did Mr. Hansard want to remove Mr. Collins from his will?"

"He wouldn't tell me the specifics. Just something about lack of loyalty."

"Were there problems between the two men?"

"Not that I'm aware of, but it's a big house, and I'm rarely in the same room as the others. My job keeps me quite busy."

"Do you think Jared or Jessica might have found out they're no longer in the will?"

"Oh, no. Definitely not. If they had, the entire town would have heard. Besides, to the best of my knowledge, the only people who know about the will are Mr. Hansard's lawyer and me."

Mary Smith had jumped right from person of interest to number one suspect. "What about Mr. Corbin? Any conflict with him?"

"I don't believe so. Mr. Corbin's done a lovely job on the landscape and maintaining it. Mr. Hansard enjoyed sitting in his gardens, admiring his yard. He was quite pleased with Mr. Corbin's work."

"Mary, why do you think Mr. Hansard would put you in his will but not his living relatives?"

She rubbed her hands together again. That must have been how she released energy when she felt anxious or nervous. "Loyalty and devotion were very important to Mr. Hansard. I guess he thought I was a loyal and devoted employee. I didn't ask for the money, if that's what you're suggesting, and I only found out a few days ago, when he told me he wanted to remove Mr. Collins. Like I said, I made the call to his lawyer to get the process going."

"Have you ever played the game Clue?"

She blinked. "The board game? Maybe years ago. I'm not sure."

"I played it as a kid all the time. I loved how the cards determined the killer, location, and the murder weapon. You know, in his office, by his butler, with a gun."

She furrowed her brow. "I'm not sure I understand why you're telling me this."

"It's kind of like a game of Clue, Mr. Hansard's murder. We have a house full of suspects, and to find the killer, we just have to pick the right cards."

"I still don't know what you're trying to say."

"Just that this situation made that connection for me, that's all." I wanted to give the illusion that she was safe from being my primary suspect so she wouldn't try to run—all while implying I knew the killer was still in the house. "Thank you, Ms. Smith. I'd like you to go back and wait with the others, but please keep our conversation private."

"Yes, ma'am."

I found Ashley outside of Mr. Hansard's office. "Has anyone found any house keys on him?"

Dr. Barron shifted his head from Mr. Hansard's remains to me. "I've checked all his pockets. No keys. None around his desk either. Ashley, come on in and have a look." He stood and removed his gloves. "I'm finished here." He met me just outside the office. "Looks like you've got yourself a homicide."

3

"Kind of already thought that," I said with a smile. "And I have a primary suspect already."

"I don't doubt that."

"Did you find the bullet?"

He shook his head. "I suspect Ashley will find it somewhere in the bookcase, but I'll be honest, I didn't look."

"I'd like to pick nine-millimeter for a thousand."

Barron's eyes shifted to me. "That's funny. I was thinking more like the butler, in the study, with a gun."

I laughed. "I said something similar earlier to Michels. He didn't get it, but I think Mary Smith did."

"Michels is still green."

Bishop walked up. "Ryder." He crooked his finger and flicked his head for me to follow him.

"When will you do the autopsy?" I asked Dr. Barron.

He checked his watch. "Probably first thing in the morning. I'll let you know."

"Thanks, Doc." I followed Bishop into a room I couldn't name.

He closed the door behind us. "I've interviewed Jessica. She's a fun one."

"I think the house five acres away heard her scream."

We compared stories. Jessica's was like what Mary said. "She was in her room. Said she was getting ready to go out for dinner."

"Where's her room?" I asked.

"Far hall up to the right. Last room on the left."

"She had to have booked it downstairs, then," I said.

"She's young. She probably can," Bishop said.

"Mary Smith is getting money from Hansard's will. She and a retirement home or something. Jared and Jessica aren't in the will."

"Really? Do they know that?" he asked.

"According to Mary, she's the only one who knows."

"So we have a housekeeper who probably spends the most time with the victim and who stands to receive a lot of money if her boss dies. I'm thinking that's a good motive for murder," he said.

"Right, but we still have to do our due diligence. Let's talk with the butler and the lawn guy. And I'm still thinking Jared is a possibility. Let's let him sweat it out a bit for a while. I feel like he's the guy with the information we're missing. Which do you want?"

"What should we do? Rock, paper, scissors?"

I laughed.

"I'll take the butler," he said.

"Works for me," I said, and we returned to the room with the suspects.

Michels met us in the hall. "All windows and doors have been checked. None were unlocked or broken. None looked messed with either. Looks like an inside job."

"I want my attorney!" Jessica screamed.

"Michels," I said. "Get her on the phone with the attorney, please. But be prepared. He or she is going to turn her down, and she's going to lose it."

"How do you know?"

"I know things," I said. I winked and walked into the room. "Mr. Corbin?"

He'd been pacing the length of the floor with his head down. He glanced up and pointed at himself. "Me?"

"Are there any other Mr. Corbins in the house?" I asked.

He blushed. "No, ma'am."

He followed me into another room.

Michels came by before we closed the door. "Left a message with the attorney's answering service."

"Thanks." I smiled at Mr. Corbin. "Have a seat." I sat across from him. He picked at his nails. He'd pulled his long, dishwater-blond hair into a bun on the top of his head. It appeared he'd run out of shampoo months ago. "How long have you worked for Mr. Hansard?"

"Two years."

"And what exactly did you do for him?"

He bounced in his chair. "Lawn maintenance. Planting, upkeep, moving, that kind of stuff."

"Do you have a key to the house?"

He narrowed his eyes. "Uh, no. Why would I need that?"

"Where were you when you heard the shot fired?"

"Out back. I was getting ready to plant the flowers he requested. You can look and see."

"Tell me what happened."

"Not much to tell. I was out prepping the garden at the patio. I heard the shot, ran inside, and saw Mr. Collins and Jared standing near Mr. Hansard." I watched as his Adam's apple bounced up and down his neck. "There was a lot of blood. I just, you know. I couldn't handle it, so I walked away. Next thing I knew, the cop was at the front door."

"Where did you go?"

"Just over near the front door. I needed some fresh air. I've seen nothing like that before."

"Did you call anyone?"

He shook his head. "I checked my voicemail. Just needed to keep busy, I guess." He stood. "I can show you my phone."

As he reached into his pocket, I said, "Not now. Please, sit, and keep your hands away from your pockets."

"Oh, yeah," he said as he clasped his hands together. "Sorry."

"Mr. Corbin, why did you test positive for gunpowder residue on your hands?"

He blinked. "I, uh, I cleaned my weapon last night."

"What kind of weapon do you own?"

"A Luger."

"Do you own any other weapons?"

"No, ma'am."

"You were the last one to get to Mr. Hansard's office."

He nodded. "The back door was locked, so I had to go around to the front."

"Was the front door unlocked?"

"Yes, ma'am."

"Did anyone say anything about what happened?"

"Not that I can recall," he said. "Miss Jessica had already begun pitching a fit, but she does that just about every day. I think Mr. Collins and Jared were arguing, but I'm not sure what about. Ms. Smith was in the office checking Mr. Hansard's pulse, and that's when I left."

"Okay. Do you know of any issues Mr. Hansard was having with family, or friends, or even enemies?"

"No, ma'am. We talk about what he needs done in the yard. That's it. He shares nothing personal with me."

"Has he ever mentioned his will?"

"No, ma'am. Like I said, he doesn't share personal stuff."

"Understood. Do you know where the others were prior to the shooting?"

"I can't say for sure."

"Do you know of anyone who had any conflict with Mr. Hansard?"

"Well, when I think about it, everyone has at one point or another. He's kind of a cranky old man."

"What about the butler?"

"Not that I can think of, but that doesn't mean he hasn't. Like I said, he's a cranky old man."

"The housekeeper?"

"Okay, so her, maybe not. She's been with him a long time, and I've never heard them argue. So, no. I don't think so. She and Mr. Hansard seem pretty tight. She's always doting on him, doing everything he asks even if it's not part of her job."

"Do you know why she does that?" I asked.

He shrugged. "She's a nice lady?"

A nice lady who might have committed murder. I stood. "I'd like you to stick around in the room with the others."

"Do I need an attorney?"

I raised an eyebrow. "Do you *think* you need an attorney?"

He shrugged. "I'm not a suspect, am I?"

"Mr. Corbin, everyone is a suspect until they aren't."

4

"Collins said he and Jared fought about leaving Hansard alone," Bishop said. "He worried about damaging the crime scene, but Jared didn't want his grandfather being there like that without family."

"How very kind of him," I said. "I asked Michels to check Corbin's phone. He said he checked his voicemail. He also said he couldn't get in the back door, so he had to go around to the front."

"Was it open?" he asked.

I nodded.

"Great." Bishop rubbed the side of his face, then dragged his hand to his chin and rubbed it as well. "That means the killer could have come in, shot Hansard, then left."

"The thought crossed my mind. Did Collins say if anyone had any beef with the deceased?"

"The usual family problems the rich always seem to have. Hansard threatened the kids by dangling the money over their heads."

"What about other employees?"

Bishop shook his head. "Didn't mention anything about

them or himself. Said everyone kept to their jobs, so there weren't any problems. We interviewing the grandson together?"

I smiled. "Technically it's his great-grandson."

"You know what I mean."

"I do, and yes, I think questioning Hansard's great-grandson together is an excellent idea."

Someone knocked on the door. Then it inched open, and Jared peeked inside through the small crack. "Is anyone going to talk to me?"

Bishop swung the door open and held it ajar for Jared Hansard. "We were just coming to get you."

Jared stormed past Bishop and stood in front of me with his hands on his hips. "I didn't kill my great-grandfather." He ran his hand through his short dark hair. "I swear."

"Thanks for the information," Bishop said.

"Listen, I know what those a-holes think of me. I know they're trying to frame me for this."

"What makes you think he was murdered?" I asked.

He blinked. "I mean, he was shot in the eye. It's not like he did it himself."

Was the kid a criminal justice expert? He did have a point. "No one has accused anyone of anything."

"Oh yeah? Then why haven't you talked to me yet? Why everyone else?"

"Like I said, we were just coming to get you," Bishop said.

"What did the others say?" he asked. He ran his hand through his hair again.

Jared Hansard was an attractive kid. I suspected those good looks and his family money allowed him to get away with things most people couldn't. Possibly even murder. "Where were you when you heard the shot?"

"I was upstairs in my room."

"What did you do after you heard it?" Bishop asked.

"I ran downstairs to see what happened."

Bishop continued with his line of questions. "Who was there when you got there?"

"Uh, Collins. Ms. Smith arrived and checked my great-grandfather's pulse, but I'd already done that. I told her he was dead. I told Collins the same thing. He called 911 and wanted me to get away from my great-grandfather, but I wouldn't leave him like that."

"Mr. Collins was in the office with you?" I asked.

He nodded. "He was there when I came downstairs."

"And he walked into the hallway to call 911?"

"He called from the office. I don't know why he thought I should leave but he could stick around. He's the butler. I'm blood."

"I understand you and your great-grandfather have had some issues," Bishop said. "Tell us about those."

"I mean, yeah. We had issues. He's old and never leaves the house. He has no idea how the world is today. He thinks I should follow these old-fashioned rules, but that's not how things work anymore. But it wasn't like we fought all the time. Now Jess, they battled it out daily."

"What did they argue about?" Bishop asked.

"Everything. Like I said, he's old-fashioned. He didn't think Jess should show all that skin, go on dates with different guys, bring them home to her room, all that stuff. Last week when she walked a guy out, he told her if she brought home another one, he'd kick her out."

"How did she respond to that?" I asked.

"Like she always responds. Screaming and crying. Jess thinks if she cries loud enough, she'll get what she wants."

"Does she?"

He exhaled. "Usually, but just because we all want her to shut up."

"Jared," I said. "Where do you work?"

His eyes widened. "I don't. I live off my trust fund."

I nodded once. "A trust fund from your great-grandfather?"

"Yes."

"How did he feel about that?" I asked.

"Yeah, he wasn't happy, but it's not like I'm never going to work. I just want to have some fun before I take life seriously."

He'd be starting that sooner rather than later. "Did you two argue about money?"

He shrugged. "What family doesn't?"

"Did Mr. Hansard threaten to take you out of his will?" I asked.

"Yeah," he said. He laughed nervously. "But he wouldn't do that. I mean, yeah, he's an asshole, but he's not that big of one, you know?"

The kid had a big surprise coming to him.

"When was the last time you spoke to your great-grandfather?" Bishop asked.

"Few days ago, I guess."

They lived in the same house but didn't speak daily? I'd grown up in a small duplex in Chicago. I spoke to my neighbors daily, let alone my family. Maybe in a mansion it was easier to ignore people? "Did you argue then?"

He glanced to the right, then looked down at his shoes. "Yes, ma'am."

"About what?" Bishop asked.

"My lack of employment." He pinched the bridge of his nose. "Fine, my great-grandfather and I weren't on the best of terms, but I didn't kill him."

"What do you think happened?" Bishop asked.

"I think you should talk to Collins about that. He was the first in the room, and when I got there, he was standing over my great-grandfather, so you tell me."

"Did Mr. Collins have issues with your grandfather?" I asked.

"Everyone had issues with him. He wasn't a nice guy. He expected everyone to do what he wanted and do it his way. He threatened us constantly, and if we didn't do what he wanted, he'd punish us."

"Did he punish you?"

"Which time?" He laughed.

"The last time you argued."

"Nah, but he probably hadn't gotten around to it. One time took the keys to my Tesla, but I'm not an idiot. I have three sets because I knew he'd pull that shit on me eventually."

"What about Mr. Collins?" Bishop asked. "Had he threatened him in any way?"

He nodded. "A few days, maybe a week or so ago? I can't remember exactly. I was in the kitchen, and he called Collins into his office. At first, I didn't hear anything, but his voice got louder and louder. I'm pretty sure everyone heard it."

Bishop nodded. "What was the discussion about?"

"Collins had asked for time off, and good ol' great-grandfather Jeremiah said no. When Collins told him why he wanted it, all hell broke loose. Jeremiah said Collins's loyalty should be to him first."

"Why did Collins want the time off?" Bishop asked.

"His daughter just had a baby. His first grandchild. He wanted to fly out to Texas to see her. He asked for a week off. The poor guy hasn't had a week off since I can remember."

"Jared, do you own a gun?" I asked.

He blinked. "Yes, ma'am."

"What kind?"

"A Luger."

"A Luger what?" Bishop asked.

"A Luger. You know, a Luger gun."

If the kid didn't know what kind of Luger he owned, it was likely he had no idea how to shoot it either. Someone shot Hansard at close range, something a novice could do if they'd kept their hand steady enough to hit the target.

"We're going to need to see your gun," I said.

"It's in my bedroom," he said.

I asked Michels to escort Jared to his room to retrieve the gun. "Oh, Jared, one more thing. Do you know where everyone was at the time of the shooting?"

"You mean like in the house?"

I nodded.

"No clue."

5

Bishop and I talked through what we knew. "The children," Bishop said, "don't have a specific motive unless they were aware of Hansard's decision to remove them from the will."

"Specific motive that we know of. But you're right about the will. Ms. Smith said if they knew, the entire town would have heard about it. Given how Jessica's reacted today, I believe her."

Bishop nodded. "I can't see Jessica pulling the trigger."

Bishop had a soft spot for women. He struggled to believe them capable of heinous crimes, but it was my experience that women were nastier than men. "Don't count her out. She and her great-uncle had words about her easy-with-the-men lifestyle. He threatened to kick her out if she brought another man home."

"She failed to mention that," Bishop said.

"What? A girl tried to manipulate a situation. Shocker!"

He rolled his eyes. "Jared Hansard came in on the defensive. That causes pause."

"I don't disagree with that, but my gut tells me it's not him," I said.

"Why does your gut think that?" he asked.

"He hadn't seen his grandfather in a few days. I get the impression he stayed clear of him to not cause conflict so he wouldn't have his trust fund pulled out from under him."

"He could be lying about when they spoke last."

I nodded. "If he is, we'll find out. Back to Jessica. If she had men in and out of the mansion, it's possible one of them did it and took off."

"Michels checked the security cameras. The only person who came in since this morning was Corbin, and that coincided with the time of the murder."

"No one told me they had security cameras."

"I assumed you saw them at the front door," Bishop said.

I chided myself for being so wrapped up in the monstrosity of a house I failed to see something so obvious. "What about cameras in other areas?"

"Let's get him in here." He called Michels in.

"Detective Ryder," Michels said. "We tagged Jared Hansard's weapon for evidence. It was where he said he put it."

"Thanks for helping on that," I said.

"No problem."

"What about the rest of the security cameras?" Bishop asked.

"All but one in working order," Michels responded.

"Which one isn't working?" Bishop asked.

"Center one near double doors to the patio out back."

Bishop and I eyed each other.

"Is it where Corbin was working?" I asked.

"Yes, ma'am."

"Can you bring him to us?" Bishop asked.

"Yes, sir."

I chewed on my bottom lip. "It's possible he could have

snuck inside, shot Hansard, then rushed back outside and played dumb. Based on where everyone was, he wouldn't have run into anyone."

"But why? What's his motive?"

"That's what we have to figure out."

~

AN HOUR LATER, we'd landed on two possible suspects from the group but chose to keep that information from them. We needed them to stick around because we knew once we left the house, they'd all be gone, and we'd get nothing out of them.

"Why do we have to stay?" Ms. Smith asked. "I don't understand."

"We can't allow anyone to leave just yet," Bishop said. "Not until we get more information."

While Bishop discussed the generalities of policing a murder crime scene, I watched the group react. Hansard's murderer had either acted out of anger or planned it exactly as it had played out. If I were a gambler, I'd have bet it was planned that way. Why? Because it would seem illogical to the average person to plan and execute a murder with several other people in the home. The risk would be too great, and that was exactly what the killer would want. To make the murder seem illogical, therefore something other than planned. Effectively making it impossible for people to believe it was him or her that committed the crime.

I studied each of the suspects, starting with Jared Hansard. He leaned against a wall, the top of his head tipped back. His eyes were closed, his hands stuffed into his pockets. He was frustrated, and getting impatient, all opposite signs of a killer. Killers focused hard on staying calm. They didn't want to give anything that might make them look guilty.

Jessica Hansard continued to sniffle into a tissue, but as she did, she looked at everyone else in the room. Her eyes settled on Jimmy Corbin for a few seconds longer than the others. A quick glance his direction told me Corbin made eye contact with her.

Interesting.

Mary Smith sat in a chair in the corner of the room, distancing herself from the others as I suspected she had in her job as well. She twisted a tissue in her hand while her eyes focused on Bishop. Thomas Collins stood straight, his shoulders back, and his hands folded in front of him. He'd probably stood that way for years and it had become a habit. He watched Bishop with a blank face.

"Mr. Collins," I said after Bishop finished. "Come with us, please."

The rest of the group gawked at him as he walked to us, but he didn't flinch. We met with him in another room.

"Congratulations," Bishop said.

He pursed his lips. "For?"

"On being a grandparent," I said. "Too bad Hansard wouldn't give you the time off to meet your grandchild."

"Who told you that?" he asked.

"A little birdie," Bishop said. "That birdie also said you argued with Hansard about it."

His upper lip twitched. "It was a discussion, not an argument, and he allowed me the time off. I'm scheduled to leave tomorrow."

"Got anything to verify that?" I asked.

"A plane ticket paid for by Mr. Hansard. I have the receipt to prove it." He took a breath and released it. "When I first approached Mr. Hansard, he refused my time off. Did I get upset? Yes, of course. Beebee is my first grandchild. Who would deny a grandfather time with his daughter and his granddaughter?"

"Apparently, Mr. Hansard," I said.

"As I said, we discussed it. It didn't end well, so perhaps that is what your little birdie told you. Mr. Hansard threatened to fire me if I left."

"How did he go from threatening to fire you to buying your ticket?" Bishop asked.

"Many don't see it, but Mr. Hansard is a fair man. He realized he was overreacting, and he chose to buy the ticket to apologize for his behavior. Gave it to me a few hours after we argued."

"He tell you that? That he was sorry?" I asked.

"He didn't have to. I've worked for him long enough to know how he operates. He would never apologize. It's not his character. But he does show remorse in other ways."

"Like buying the ticket," Bishop said.

"And buying his great-grandson a Tesla, and his great-grandniece a Mercedes."

"How did Mr. Hansard feel about his niece?" Bishop asked.

"He never said, but he didn't have to. His expressions made his feelings clear. He was disappointed in her. She lived a flamboyant lifestyle in his eyes. Too much of everything, but mostly, too many men. He comes from a different era. Living freely as she does doesn't make sense to him."

"Did you see these men?"

"Several, yes, but I assume I missed many as well."

"Were there any men here during the last few days?"

"Not that I can recall, which is unusual, actually. She stayed home most of the past week as well."

"That's not normal for her?"

"Not at all. She treats this home as a luxury hotel. She

comes and goes as she pleases, expects food, clean linens and clothing, and demands her privacy. This past week, she's stayed home."

"Any idea why?" I asked.

He shook his head. "She doesn't speak to the help unless she needs something."

"Have you seen anyone new come to the home recently?" Bishop asked.

"No one other than delivery companies have come of late."

"What's your relationship with Ms. Smith?" I asked.

"One of mutual respect, I would hope. We are friendly, but that's about it. We all tend to keep to ourselves and do our work. Mr. Hansard is quite demanding of things being a certain way."

"The same with Mr. Corbin?"

"Yes, ma'am. We have only spoken a handful of times. He's outside when here. It's hard to have any conversation when we're in opposite areas of the property."

"Have you seen him with Jessica Hansard?" I asked.

Bishop shot me a questioning look with a raised eyebrow.

"Not that I'm—as a matter of fact, I did see them talking outside yesterday."

"Is that unusual?" I asked. He'd already told me Jessica didn't speak to the help, but asking the same questions in different ways often got different answers.

"As I said, she doesn't normally speak to us. Perhaps she had some concerns about the plant choices. You'd have to ask them."

Bishop and I made eye contact. "Do you know where everyone was in the house before the shooting?"

"I'm not sure. I think I saw Jared and Mr. Hansard in his office, but I could be remembering wrong."

"What about Mary Smith?"

"I don't know."

Bishop nodded and stood. "Thank you, Mr. Collins. I'll walk you out."

"Will I be able to visit my daughter and granddaughter still?" he asked.

"We'll keep you posted," Bishop said.

6

Talking to Jessica was like talking to a toddler whose toy you'd taken away. I dragged my fingers over my eyes and waited for her to stop bawling. She wasn't crying because her great-uncle died. She cried because she'd received a message from her attorney.

"Why did he do this to me?" She'd been escorted to her room immediately after hearing from the attorney to retrieve a file. She handed it to me. "See? It's all here! I was in the will two weeks ago! Can I contest it? Can't I go to court or something? He can't just change it like that."

"Actually, he can," I said. "It's his money to do with as he pleases." I briefly reviewed the out-of-date will. She had been left three million dollars. I wondered if it would have been enough.

"But I'm homeless now."

"Jessica," Bishop said. "How did you get a copy of the will?"

She swallowed hard. "Jared gave it to me."

"He has one as well?" he asked.

"Well, yeah, obviously."

"When did he give it to you?"

"I already told you. Two weeks ago. How could it change without me knowing? Aren't I supposed to be notified or something?"

It must be interesting, living in a fantasy world like that.

"Jessica," Bishop said. He kept his voice steady and calm. "Why would your great-uncle remove you from the will?"

She sniffled. "He wouldn't. He promised he'd take care of me. We had an agreement."

"An agreement?" I asked.

She nodded. "He wouldn't take me out of the will if I stopped bringing men home. And I did. I have. I've barely gone anywhere over the past week! Why would he do this? I gave up my fun for that money, and now I've got nothing!"

Jessica didn't know about the will change. She hated changing her lifestyle but needed the cash to live. That was her motive. Kill Hansard, get the cash, and live the easy life with all the men she wanted. I caught Bishop's eye. He nodded once. He'd been thinking the same thing.

"Do you know where everyone was before the gunshot?"

"I know I was in my room. I don't pay much attention to the help."

Nice.

We asked her a few more questions which got us nowhere. I finally asked, "Did you kill your great-uncle?"

Her jaw dropped to the floor. Sobs soared from her mouth as her eyes darkened and shot arrows directly at me. "How dare you say that! I might be a lot of things, but I am not a murderer!" She dropped her head into her hands and cried more.

Bishop eyed at me with a look that said, *Do something.* What did he expect me to do? I wasn't a miracle worker. "Jessica," I said. I touched her shoulder. She jerked away. "We need you to calm down. You're not being charged with anything. We're simply trying to understand what happened."

She looked up from her hands. "What happened?" She breathed through her nose, and it made a whistling sound. "My great-uncle was murdered and took me out of the will, that's what happened!"

Thanks for stating the obvious.

"Jessica," Bishop said. I figured he could see my eyes rolling at her drama. God knew I could feel them. "Were you aware of any issues anyone might have had with your great-uncle?"

She laughed. "Everyone has issues with my him. In case you didn't know, he's a jerk. He respects no one and thinks he's better than all of us. He used to make fun of Jim—Mr. Corbin all the time. He laughed because he's in lawn maintenance, but he's more than that. He has a master's in horticulture. He used to work for the Atlanta Botanical Garden. He designed the specialty gardens."

"Are you and Mr. Corbin friends?" I asked.

She looked to the right and then to the ground. "No. He's old."

Right.

"Is it possible Mr. Corbin heard the things your great-uncle said about him, got angry, and decided to kill him?"

She looked me in the eye. "Why would he do that? That's crazy. He'd lose his job. He needs this job."

Clearly there was something going on with Jessica and Jimmy. But was it something that would drive one of them to murder?

"Are you in a relationship with Mr. Corbin?" Bishop asked.

She blinked. "No. Gross."

"Are you sure?" I asked. "I'm old too, but I remember being your age, and I know what it's like to crush on an older guy."

That was a lie. I'd never crushed on an older guy, and even if I had, I wouldn't have chosen those words. I just tried to talk her talk.

She twisted the tissue in her hands until it pulled in two.

"Jessica, you can lie to us now, but when we find out, and we will, it's going to look bad for you. If you tell us the truth now, things will go a lot easier."

She exhaled. "Fine. Yes, we're together. We're in love, okay? We just didn't want my great-uncle to know. He would have fired Jimmy and kicked me out."

"Did anyone else know?" Bishop asked.

"What? No. I told you, I don't speak to anyone here. I can't stand this place. It's so old, and gross, and it smells."

My patience thinned. "How long have you been with Mr. Corbin?"

"A few weeks, but we've been flirting for a few months."

A few weeks was about the time the will changed. I nodded once to Bishop. He and I had just begun reading each other's facial expressions, so he got my nod.

"That's all for now," he said.

"Am I free to go?"

"No, ma'am. You're free to stick around. We'll be with you again soon."

After she left, I said, "Interesting how neither of them told us the little nugget about Jared having acquired the will."

"Isn't it?" He dragged his hand down his chin. His five o'clock shadow had grown into a ten o'clock one. "Did any of your interviews confirm Mr. Corbin was outside before Hansard was shot?"

"Nope."

"Let's ask again, just in case," he said.

Five minutes later we had our answer. It was the same as before. No one had seen Jimmy Corbin outside. No one could verify his whereabouts at the time of the murder. Mr. Collins even said he didn't know Corbin was there until after the incident.

"The front door was open," Bishop said. "Unlocked. That could have given Corbin time to walk in, shoot Hansard, then walk out, and quickly rush in like he'd been working out back."

"Right. The problem is, they all have gunpowder on their hands, so how do we prove that?"

"First, we get Michels checking his vehicle."

So, we did.

And we weren't surprised at what we'd found.

"It's been shot recently," Bishop said. He held the Luger in his gloved hands.

"The timing works," I said.

"Corbin says it's not his weapon. He said his is at home."

"Hansard is missing a weapon in his safe."

"But how do we explain gunpowder on Collins, Jared, and Jessica Hansard? And what's the motive?"

"The motive is easy. Corbin or Jessica found out she'd been removed from the will. Maybe Corbin is so blinded by love, he sought revenge for hurting his girlfriend?"

"Anything's possible," Bishop said. "Gunpowder?"

"Collins and Jared were in the office. They could have touched something and got it on their hands. Jessica..." I had to think about that one. "Jessica touched Corbin, and it came off on her."

"A good lawyer would say she touched any of the others and got it from them. We need something more than that."

It was past midnight. We were tired. The house staff was tired, and we'd come up with nothing. "Should we sit on this?"

I asked. "We still have Mary Smith as a top suspect. Maybe we need to let these people bask in their fear for a while?"

"No. We need something tonight. Someone's got to go to jail for this tonight."

He was right, damn it.

A knock on the door interrupted us. The door slowly opened, and Mary Smith peeked through. "I'm sorry to bother you, but I need to get home. My daughter is having a rough night, and I need to be there to help her."

"I'm sorry," Bishop said. "We can't clear anyone to leave right now. I'm sure your daughter will understand."

Her hopeful eyes dropped. "No, she won't. My daughter suffers from autism. She's noncommunicative. She doesn't understand much. Her caregiver asked for me to come home. I'm not usually here at this hour, and I can't force her to stay."

"I'm very sorry," Bishop said again. "But we can't release you just yet."

"How old is your daughter?" I asked.

"She's nineteen. Her father left us after her diagnosis. He said it was too much work. I've been caring for her with the help of other caregivers since, but I can't do much more. She's too big, and I can't lift her like I used to. I'm going to need to move her into a care facility."

"That must be hard," I said. What I thought was that it must be expensive. The girl was nineteen. She could live another sixty years, and if there wasn't money to care for her, she'd become a ward of the state. God only knew what that meant. "Have you found a place?" I asked.

She nodded. "The Sunshine House."

That was the place mentioned in Mr. Hansard's will. Good old Mary Smith cemented her position at the top of my suspect list.

"Oh, that's in town," Bishop said. "Great place. Their staff is dedicated."

"I hope so," she said. "If you'll excuse me, I need to call my caregiver and beg her to stay."

As she closed the door, I said, "It's her, Bishop. She did it."

He shook his head. "I'm still not sure. She's too..." He let that trail off to nothing.

"Money is a big motive. The will says outside of the two million that goes to her, all money goes to The Sunshine House. That was the place I thought was a retirement home or something." I hesitated, then said what had just popped into my mind. "It's not just the money. It's her daughter. She needs to make sure her daughter is cared for. I think she changed his will to say she gets the money, and then she forged his signature, and when the will came back from the lawyer, she waited for the right opportunity and killed him."

"How can you prove that?"

"She said she's his house manager. She pays his bills. It's not a leap to think she could have forged his signature."

"But he'd need a witness to watch him sign the will and have it notarized."

"She is the witness, and what's saying the attorney didn't just have it notarized after the fact, since Hansard is a wealthy client and a shut-in?" I bounced in my seat. "And she had access to the gun. The Luger missing from the safe. It's the one planted in Corbin's trunk. She killed Hansard, then ran outside and placed the weapon in the trunk."

"Because she needs the money now, not when Hansard kicked the bucket naturally."

"Yes," I said.

"Hell."

"Right there with you," I said.

Jessica screamed down the hall. "Oh, my God! She's got a gun!"

I retrieved my weapon as we raced to the room and skidded to a stop when we saw Mary Smith holding a gun mere millimeters from Jared Hansard's head. "Don't come any closer, or I'll shoot!" Her finger rested on the trigger. Any move by us would be lost to her reflexes and her finger's proximity to a pull.

"Mary," Bishop said. He pointed his weapon at her. "Put the gun down. Let's have a conversation."

"It's too late to talk!" Tears streamed down her face. "You don't understand. I had to do it! My daughter needs help! I can't do it on my own." She pressed the gun against Jared's head.

He stared at me, his eyes wide and filled with anger or fear or both. "Get this crazy bitch away from me! I don't want to die!"

"Just stay still," I said.

"Oh, my God! Oh, my God!" Jessica screamed.

Mary's nose flared. "Shut her up! I'm so tired of listening to her spoiled whining. She thinks she deserves the money?" She laughed. "What did she ever do to earn it? I busted my butt for Hansard. I cleaned his toilet and let him treat me like shit just so I could help my daughter. He knew that. He knew I'd do anything for her, and he kept dangling that in my face! You know what he did when I asked him for help? He laughed at me. He laughed when I told him I had to put my daughter in a home! He thought it was funny." She squeezed Jared's bicep. "I fucking showed him, didn't I?"

"You changed the will. You forged his signature on the paperwork and got the lawyer's office to notarize it without signing in front of them."

She laughed. "I did, and it was fucking brilliant. Now all that money belongs to me and my daughter."

I didn't let her think otherwise. I took a step closer.

"No! Don't come any closer. I'll shoot him. I have nothing to lose!"

"You have everything to lose," I said. I dropped my hand slowly to my side, then set my weapon on the floor. I held up my hands and took a step closer. "Look, I'm not going to hurt you, but I can't guarantee my partner won't. Please, just give me the gun. You don't want your daughter to end up a ward of the state, now, do you?"

She blinked. More tears fell from her eyes. She jammed the gun against Jared's head again. "Stay where you are!"

"Someone get this bitch away from me!"

Jessica screamed, "Oh, my God!" She'd been wrapped in Corbin's arms, but she pushed away from him and ran toward the couch, hitting a small table with a large glass vase on it and knocking it to the ground.

Mary Smith turned her head toward the noise, and in that split second, I charged her. Jared jumped out of the way as I dove and landed on top of Mary and tackled her to the ground. Her head hit the tile floor and made a cracking sound. Blood spread underneath her. I checked her eyes, they were still crazy-looking, so I flipped her around and cuffed her as Bishop held his gun aimed at her. He kept his foot on the inside of her knee while I locked the cuffs in place.

Jessica continued to scream. "Jessica," I yelled. "Shut up!"

Surprisingly, she stopped.

An hour later, the Hansards' attorney arrived, assuring Jessica and Jared the will would revert to the previous copy. Neither of them thanked us. I didn't expect they would.

In the vehicle on the way back to the station, I googled the game Clue. "We need to contact Hasbro."

"I'm not sure I understand," Bishop said.

"Come on, we just created the next edition of the Clue game. The housekeeper, in the office, with a gun." That game hadn't left my head since the moment we'd arrived on scene.

He laughed. "I'm surprised she didn't use a candlestick. I saw at least fifty of them around that place."

"Right?" I laughed as well. "I've never seen so much ornate, ugly crap in my life."

"Right there with you, partner."

DAMAGING SECRETS
Rachel Ryder Book 1

Bestselling author Carolyn Ridder Aspenson is back—this time with a scrappy heroine whose bold detective work and well-timed one-liners will leave you riveted—and entertained—at every turn.

New to town and a little rough around the edges, Detective Rachel Ryder finds herself on the receiving end of a suspicious person's call in Hamby, Georgia. When the call turns out to be a dead body, the medical examiner is quick to rule the death a suicide. But was it something more sinister?

Everyone in the small department believes the case is closed —except for Rachel. The sudden passing of a local politician during the mayor's run for Congress strikes her as a little too coincidental, and Rachel is eager to follow her instincts. Her partner, Rob, a 30-year veteran, isn't the type to disobey his boss or ruffle any feathers, but he can't convince strong-willed Rachel to let it go.

Obsessed with finding out the truth, Rachel begins to examine the evidence and drags her reluctant partner along for the ride. But the clues are confusing. Nothing is adding up.

Puzzled and running out of time, Rachel and Rob rush to work every angle and bring the elusive killer to justice before someone else ends up dead.

Get your copy today at
severnriverbooks.com/series/the-rachel-ryder-thrillers

ACKNOWLEDGMENTS

So many people helped get this book to publication, and I am so grateful. Severn River Publishing deserves a gold medal for managing the production of this book. A huge thank you to Julia, Amber, Mo, and Keris. You all rock! Thanks to my developmental editor, Randall Klein for guiding me through the thirty-nine page outline process and for creating the best story possible. To my other editor, Kate Schomaker, for polishing the manuscript until it shined.

As always, a big thanks to Ara Baronian, BTD Director; GPSTC, for his continued support in keeping the law enforcement details real.

And to my husband Jack for being the best thing to ever happen to me. LUMI

ABOUT CAROLYN

Carolyn Ridder Aspenson is the USA Today bestselling author of the Rachel Ryder thriller series and numerous sassy, southern cozy mysteries.

Now an empty-nester, Carolyn lives in the Atlanta suburbs with her husband, two Pit Bull-Boxer mix dogs and two cantankerous cats, but you'll often find her at a local coffee shop people-watching (and listening.) Or as she likes to call it: plotting her next novel.

Sign up for Carolyn's reader list at
severnriverbooks.com/authors/carolyn-ridder-aspenson

Printed in the United States
by Baker & Taylor Publisher Services